SEE ME RUN

I Like to Read® books, created by award-winning picture book artists as well as talented newcomers, instill confidence and the joy of reading in new readers.

We want to hear every new reader say, "I like to read!"

Visit our website for flash cards, activities, and more about the series:
www.holidayhouse.com/ILiketoRead
#ILTR

This book has been tested by an educational expert and determined to be a guided reading level D.

SEE ME RUN

Paul Meisel

I Like to Read®

HOLIDAY HOUSE • NEW YORK

For dogs and dog lovers.
And for Coco, who loves to run.

Printed and Bound in April 2018 at Tien Wah Press, Johor Bahru, Johor, Malaysia.
The artwork was created with pen and ink,
acrylic ink, and colored pencil.
www.holidayhouse.com
7 9 10 8

Library of Congress Cataloging-in-Publication Data
Meisel, Paul.
See me run / by Paul Meisel. — 1st ed.
p. cm. — (I like to read)
Summary: A dog has a fun-filled day
at the dog park, in this easy-to-read story.
ISBN 978-0-8234-2349-1 (hardcover)
[1. Dogs—Fiction. 2. Parks—Fiction.] I. Title.
PZ7.M5158752Se 2011
[E]—dc22
2010029445

ISBN 978-0-8234-2638-6 (paperback)

See me run.
I run and run.

See them come.
They come and come.

Will they get me?
No, no, no!
We go and go.

Now I stop.
What is this?

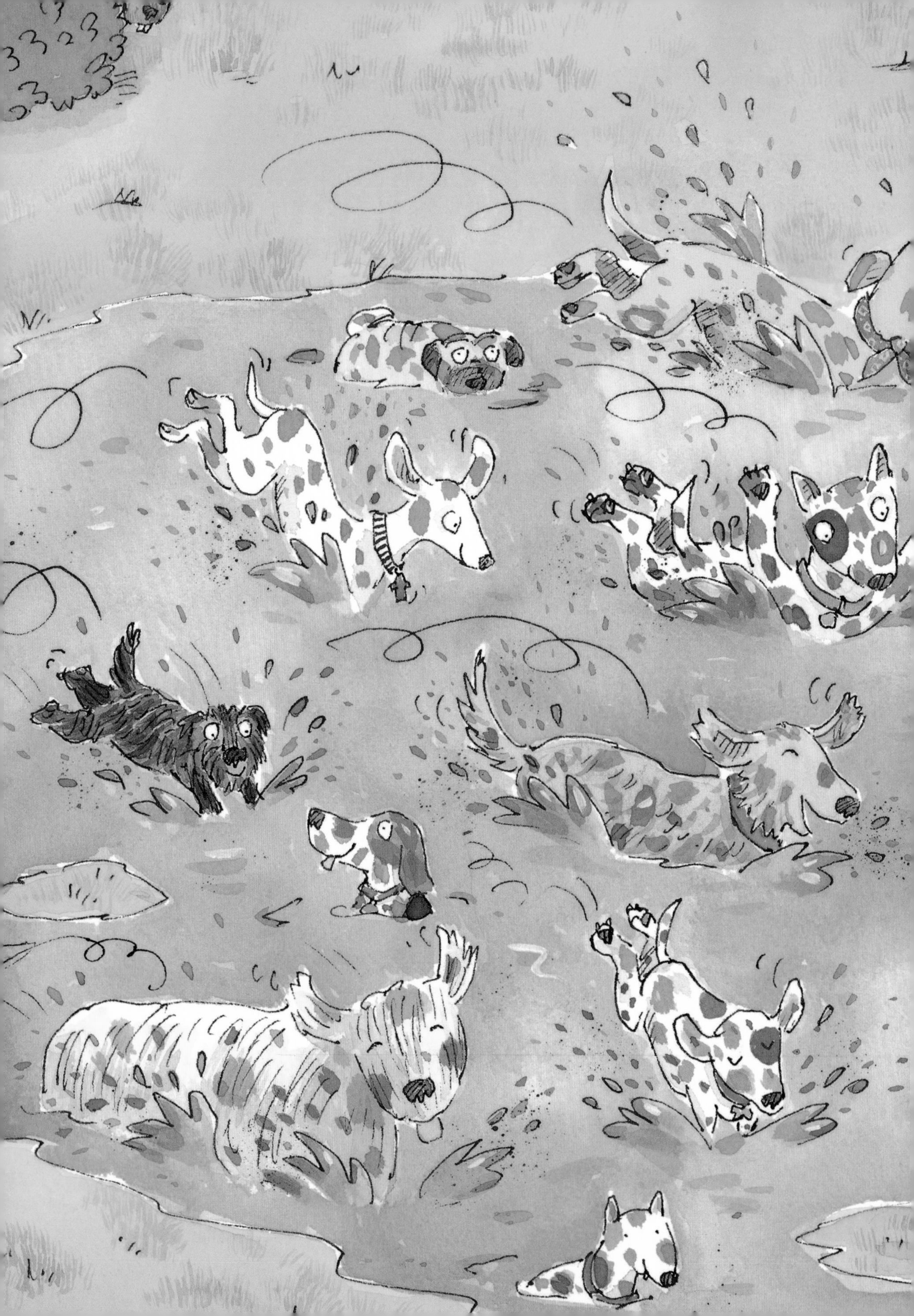

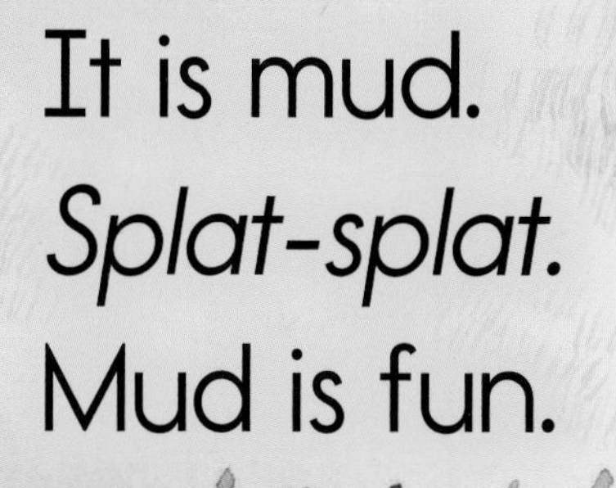

It is mud.
Splat-splat.
Mud is fun.

We need a bath.
Splash-splash.
A bath is fun.

See me dig.

We all dig.

We dig and dig and dig and dig.

What is this?

It is big.

It is mad.

And now we run again!